WITHDRAWN

D0938430

What Do Angels Wear?

Eileen Spinelli

illustrated by

Emily Arnold McCully

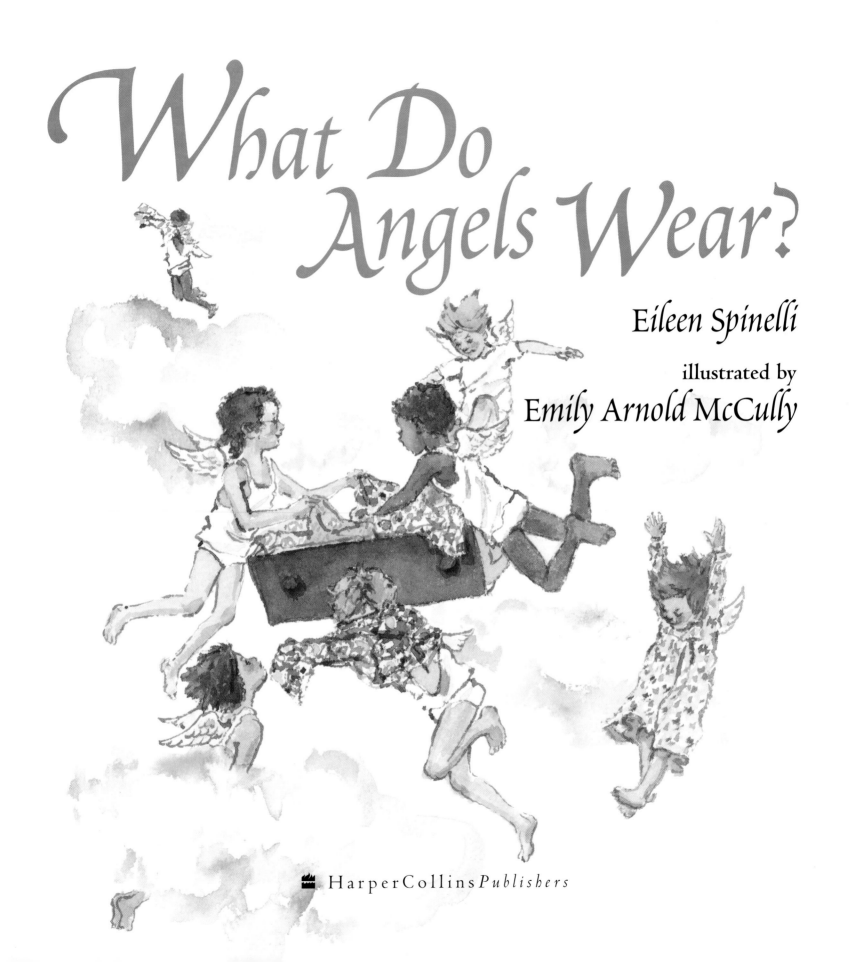

HarperCollins Publishers

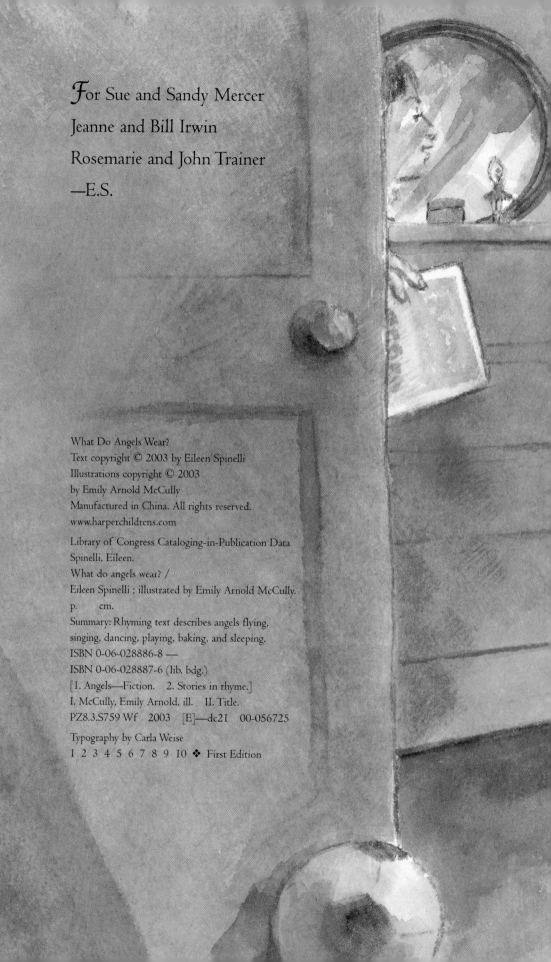

For Sue and Sandy Mercer
Jeanne and Bill Irwin
Rosemarie and John Trainer
—E.S.

What Do Angels Wear?
Text copyright © 2003 by Eileen Spinelli
Illustrations copyright © 2003
by Emily Arnold McCully
Manufactured in China. All rights reserved.
www.harperchildrens.com

Library of Congress Cataloging-in-Publication Data
Spinelli, Eileen.
What do angels wear? /
Eileen Spinelli ; illustrated by Emily Arnold McCully.
p.   cm.
Summary: Rhyming text describes angels flying,
singing, dancing, playing, baking, and sleeping.
ISBN 0-06-028886-8 —
ISBN 0-06-028887-6 (lib. bdg.)
[1. Angels—Fiction.   2. Stories in rhyme.]
I. McCully, Emily Arnold, ill.   II. Title.
PZ8.3.S759 Wf   2003   [E]—dc21   00-056725

Typography by Carla Weise
1 2 3 4 5 6 7 8 9 10 ❖ First Edition

Tell me this, can angels fly?

Yes, my dear. They sweep the sky.

They can loop with whooping crane,

Wing past windows in the rain.

*T*ell me this, can angels sing?

Yes, just like the birds in spring.

Sometimes they will sing along
With the hurdy-gurdy's song.

Tell me, what do angels wear?

They wear sparkles in their hair,

Flowing flower-printed smocks,
And in winter, woolen socks.

Tell me, do they ever dance?

Every time they get a chance!

Tango,

conga,

bunny hop,

Hula, polka—

they don't stop.

Tell me, do they like to play?

They play hide-and-seek each day.

They play wave-to-every-car.

They play Frisbee with a star.

*T*ell me this, do angels bake?

Yes. Meringues and angel cake,
Hot cross buns and scones for tea.

Every bite tastes heavenly.

Tell me, where do angels sleep?

On a cloud or in a heap,

In an orchard sweet with pears,

On benches, trains, and rocking chairs.

Tell me this, are angels real?

Yes, my love, that's how I feel.
Real as love and wind and light,

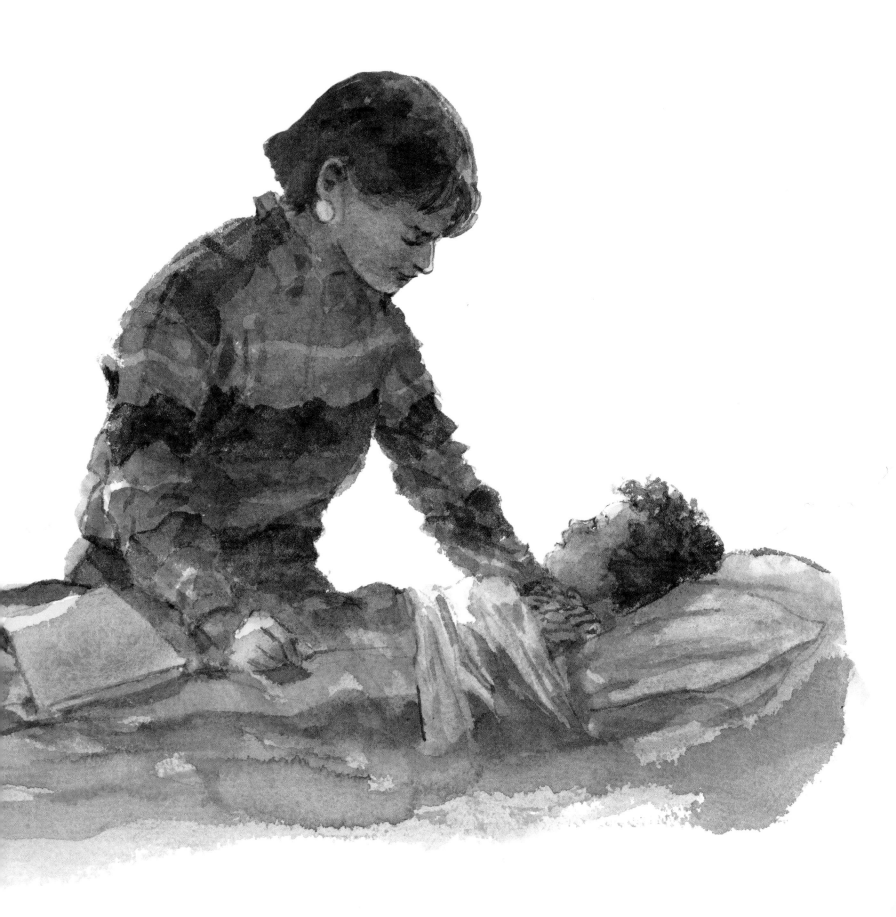

Real as Mama's kiss good night.

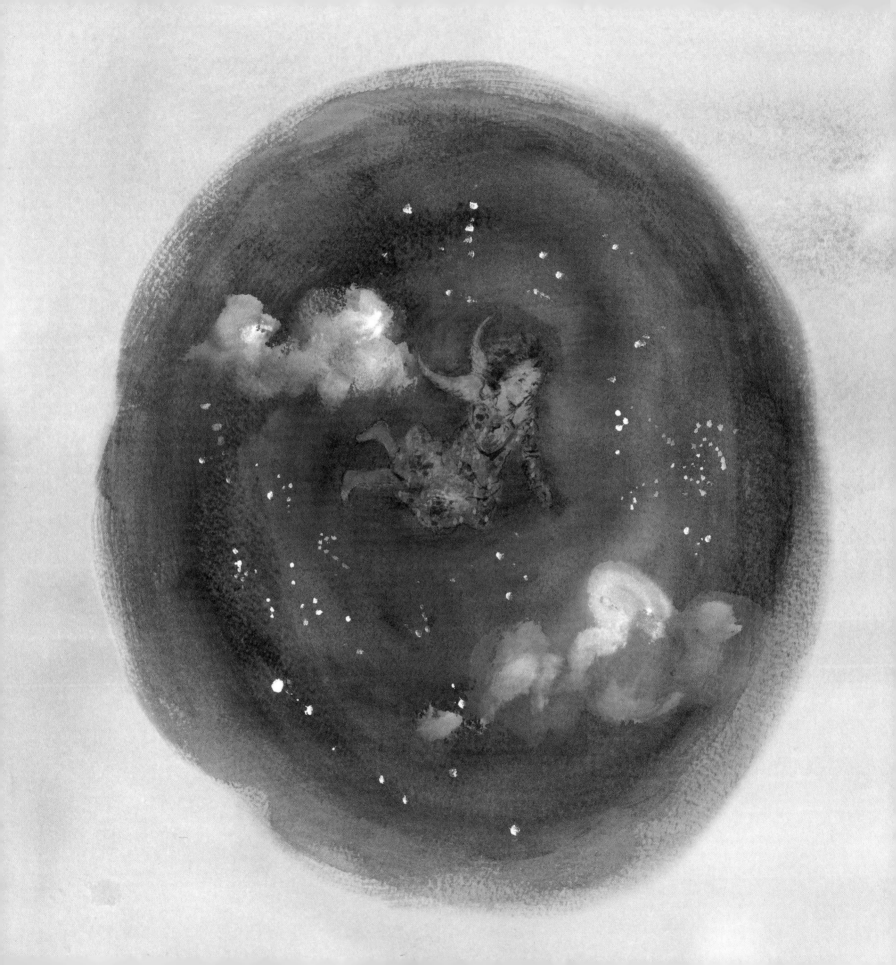